Atheneum Books for Young Readers - An imprint of Simon & Schuster Children's
Publishing Division
1230 Avenue of the Americas, New York, New York 10020
Copyright © 2004 by Vladimir Radunsky. All rights reserved, including the right of
reproduction in whole or in part in any form.
Book design by Vladimir Radunsky. Prepress by B-Side Studio Grafico, Roma
The text for this book is set in Univers Condensed, Bauer Bodoni, and Futura Extrabold.
The illustrations for this book are rendered in nice gouache on nice paper.
Manufactured in China
First Edition 10 9 8 7 6 5 4 3 2 1

Library of Congress Cataloging-in-Publication Data
Radunsky, Vladimir.
What does peace feel like? / Vladimir Radunsky.
p. cm.
"An Anne Schwartz book."
Summary: Simple text and illustrations portray what peace looks, sounds, tastes, feels,
and smells like to children around the world.
ISBN 0-689-86676-3
1. Peace–Juvenile literature. 2. Peace–Pictorial works. [1.Peace.] I. Title.
JZ5538.R33 2003
303.6'6–dc22
2003011506

care

Two percent of the publisher's net proceeds
from the sale of this book through regular
U.S. trade channels shall be donated to:

CARE
151 Ellis Street NE, Atlanta, GA 30303
http://www.careusa.org/peace

Net proceeds are the gross amounts
received by the publisher less shipping,
mailing, and insurance costs or charges and
taxes.

CARE helps communities create lasting
solutions to poverty through emergency
relief, community rehabilitation and longer-
term projects in areas such as education,
health, and small-business development.

What
PEACE

An Anne Schwartz Book
Atheneum Books for Young Readers

New York London Toronto Sydney

doES feel likE ?

by V. Radunsky
and children
just like you
from around
the world

How interesting! The word **Peace** is beautiful in all languages.

Did you ever close your eyes and try to imagine peace?

PACE

SHALOM

SALAAM

BOW-WOW
(PEACE)

PEACE

THIS dog is VERY kind, just needs A BATH

What does Peace

Like a bouquet of flowers in a happy family's living room…   like fresh and new furniture. like wind that comes in your nose when you are sleeping… like fresh air that makes you want to go out and sleep in the sun…   like pizza with onions and sausage that just came out of the oven.

smell like?

smelled by
Michael, age 10
Dario, age 8½
Finbar, age 9
Oliver, age 10
Claire, age 8

What does Peace

Like a cat and a dog
curled up together
in a basket…

like new babies just
born yesterday…

like a cloud high
up in the sky
that just happens
to be there giving
happiness to
everybody, white
and fluffy PEACE!…

like your mom
that kisses you
and hugs you…

like something beautiful
that goes away but will
come back.

look like?

seen by

Maxson, age 10

Silvia, age 8

Bruno, age 8

Giulia, age 9

Claire, age 8

What does Peace

heard by
Irene, age 8
Francesco, age 9
Irene L., age 9

Like a growling bear of war
who gets shot by a love arrow
and the fighting stops…

like a silent day…

like laughter and happiness, children on
their birthday, and parents when their
children get married…

like raindrops falling…

like everyone's heart beating, making
one big sound together…

like voices singing…

like no bad words.

sound like?

Marco, age 9

Erika, age 9

Bhavana, age 10

Fenna, age 9

What does Peace

Like vanilla ice cream, chocolate ice cream, strawberry ice cream, banana ice cream… like water… like sweet, definitely not sour… like sour, but a nice kind of sour… like your favorite food times two.

taste like?

What does Peace

Like hugs your friends give you when you cry... like the fur of my adorable cat Alice... like the fur of a baby mouse... like a lot of fun because you know you are safe... like someone stroking your back; you shiver a little, but it's a wonderful feeling.

feel like?

felt by
Tatiana, age 9 1/2
Bhavana, age 10
Fenna, age 9
Erika, age 9
Irene, age 8

Just imagine what we could build with peace.

I can't draw it all here.
A book is too small for that.

PEACE and

love to EVERYONE.

Words of Peace

Abenaki	OLAKAMIGENOKA	Greenlandic	EQQISAQATIGIINEQ	Nyanja	MTENDERE
Afrikaans	VREDE	Guarani	PYGUAPY	Otomi	HMETHO
Akkadian	SALMU	Gujarati	SHANTI	Palauan	BUDECH
Alabama	ITTIMOKLA	Halaka	PEGDUB	Pali	NIRUDHO
Albanian	PAQE	Hausa	LUMANA	Papago	DODOLIMDAG
Algonquin	WAKI IJIWEBISI	Hawaiian	MALUHIA	Pashto	AMNIAT
Alsacien	FRIEDE	Hebrew	SHALOM	Pintupi	YATANPA
Amharic	SELAM	Hiligaynon	PAGHIDAET	Polish	POKOJ
Arabic	SALAAM	Hindi	SHANTI	Portuguese	PAZ
Aranese	PATZ	Hokkien	TAI PENG	Potawatomi	ETOKMITEK
Armenian	ASHKHARH	Hopi	SHI-NU-MU	Punjabi	SHANTI
Assamese	SHANTI	Hungarian	BEKE	Pustu	SULA
Bemba	MUTENDEN	Icelandic	FRIDUR	Rapanui	KIBA KIBA
Basque	BAKEA	Igbo	UDO	Romanian	PACE
Bavarian	FRIDN	Indonesian	DAMAI	Romansch	PASCH
Batak	PARDAMEAN	Inuktitut	ANUSDAKE	Ruanda	NIMUHORE
Bengali	SHANTI	Italian	PACE	Rundi	AMAHORO
Bhojpuri	SHANTI	Japanese	HEIWA	Russian	MIR
Bislama	PIS	Javanese	TENTRAM	Saa	DAILAMA
Blackfoot	INNAIHTSIIYA	Kannada	SHANTI	Sami	RAFAIDUHHTIT
Bosnian	MIR	Kekchi	TUKTUQUIL USILAL	Samoan	FILEMU
Breton	PEOCH	Khmer	SANTEKPHEP	Sanskrit	SHANTIH
Bulgarian	MIR	Kinyarwanda	AMAHORO	Sardinian	PACHE
Buli	GOOM-JIGI	Kirundi	AMAHORO	Serbian	MIR
Burmese	NYEIN CHAN YAY	Klingon	ROJ	Setswana	KAGISO
Cantonese	PENG ON	Koasati	ILIFAYKA	Shona	RUNYARO
Carolinian	GUNNAMMWEY	Korean	PYOUNG-HWA	Sinhala	SAMAYA
Catalan	PAU	Kosati	ILIFAYKA	Sioux	WOOKEYEH
Cebuano	KALINAW	Kurdish	ASHTI	Siswati	KUTHULA
Cheyenne	NANOMONSETOTSE	Kusaiean	MIHS	Slovak	MIER
Chewa	MTENDERE	Lakota	WOWANWA	Slovenian	MIR
Choctaw	ACHUKMA	Lao	MITSUMPUN	Somali	NABAD
Chontal	AYLOBAHA GAFULEYA	Latin	PAX	Spanish	PAZ
Chuuk	KUNAMMWEY	Latvian	MIERS	Srilankan	SAAMAYA
Comanche	TSUMUKIKATU	Lingala	KIMIA	Swahili	USALAMA
Creole	PAIX	Lithuanian	TAIKA	Swedish	FRED
Crio	PIS	Lojban	PANPI	Tagalog	KAPAYAPAAN
Czech	MIR	Luganda	EMIREMBE	Tamil	SAMADAANAM
Danish	FRED	Magindanain	KALILINTAD	Tangut	NEI
Dari	SULH	Mahican	ANACHEMOWEGAN	Tatar	DUSLIK
Dutch	VREDE	Malagasi	FANDRIAMPAHALAMANA	Telugu	SHANTI
Egyptian	HETEP	Malinke	HERE	Thai	SANTIPAB
Ekari	MUKA MUKA	Maltese	PACI	Tibetan	ZHIDE
English	PEACE	Mandarin	HO-PING	Tongan	MELINO
Eskimo	ERKIGSNEK	Manobo	LINEW	Truk	KUNAMMWEY
Esperanto	PACO	Maori	RONGO	Tsalagi	NVWHTOHIYADA
Estonian	RAHU	Mapundungun	UVCHIN	Tswana	KHOTSO
Faeroese	FRIDUR	Maranao	DIAKATRA	Turkish	BARIS
Fanagolo	KUTULA	Marshallese	AENOMMAN	Turkmen	PARAHATCYLYK
Farsi	SOLH	Mentaiwan	PERDAMIAM	Twi-Akan	ASOMDWEE
Fijian	VAKACEGU	Metis Cree	PEYAHTUKE YIMOWIN	Uighur	SAQ
Finnish	RAUHA	Micmac	WONTOKODE	Urdu	AMAN
Flemish	VREDE	Miskito	KUPIA KUMI LAKA	Uzbek	TINCHLIK
Fon	FIFA	Mokilese	ONPEK	Verlent	PAXTEM
French	PAIX	Mongo	BEOTO	Vietnamese	HOA BINH
Fresian	FRED	Mossi	LAFI	Welsh	HEDD
Fula	JAM	Munsterian	ECHNAHCATON	Woleaian	GUMUND
Gaelic-Irish	SIOCHAIN	Navaho	KE	Xhosa	UXOLO
Gaelic-Scottish	SITH	Nepali	SAANTI	Yiddish	SHULAM
Galician	PAZ	Nez Perce	EYEWI	Yoruba	ALAAFIA
German	FRIEDEN	Nhengatu	TECOCATU	Yue	SAI GAAI OH PIHNG
Gikuyu	THAYU	Norwegian	FRED	Zapotec	LAYENI
Greek	EIPHNH	Ntomba	NYE	Zulu	UKUTHULA